# OPHELIA HOUSE

## PRIVATE WEDDING

ORIGINAL ARTWORK

### ANDREW L. WILLIS

CREATED AND WRITTEN

### CARLTON L. SAMPSON

COVER DESIGN, BALLOONS, PAGE LAYOUT

Palanquin

## THE BLAKE HOTEL

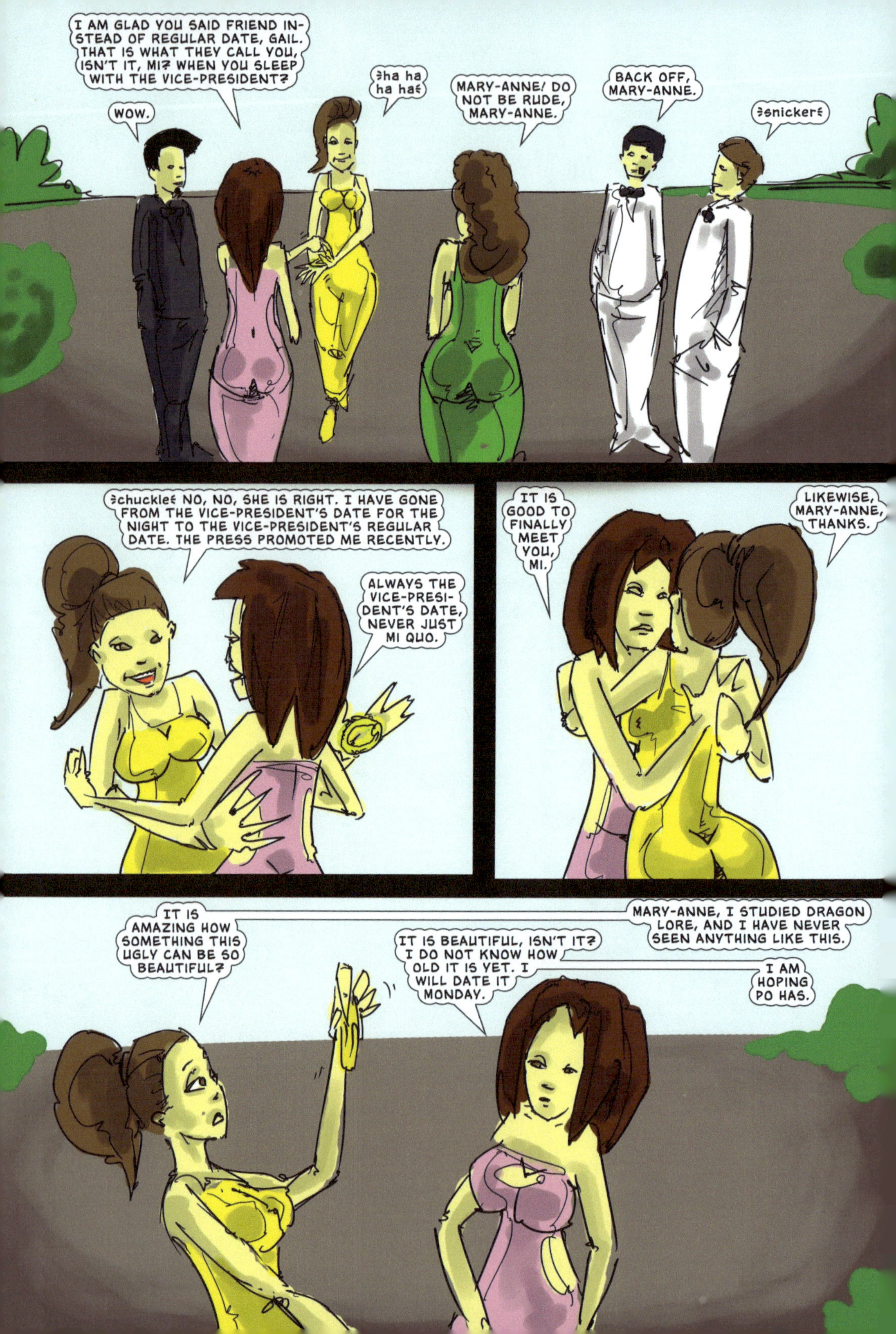

"FIRST FRIDAY" BOOK 4 PAGE 26 and "SHADOW OF THE HIVE" BOOK 7 PAGE 7

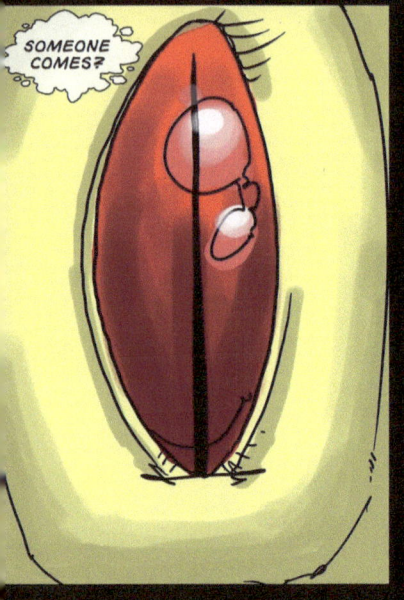

MARY-ANNE, CHARLES NEEDS TO MEET PO FIRST.
OKAY, I WILL DO THE INTRODUCTIONS.
YOU KNOW WHAT I MEAN, MARY-ANNE.
STATION MASTER CLEARED HER.
PO SEEMS HARMLESS, WILLIAM.
SEEMS HARMLESS. ARE YOU SURE SHE IS, MI?
WHAT ARE YOU WORRIED ABOUT, UNCLE WILLIAM?
YOU SAID SHE WAS UNSTABLE.
I SAID SHE WAS A SCHIZOPHRENIC MORON. I DID NOT SAY PO WAS DANGEROUS.
DOES STATION MASTER KNOW?
DOES STATION MASTER KNOW WHAT?
DOES STATION MASTER KNOW PO IS UNSTABLE?
THERE ARE BILLIONS OF HARMLESS UNSTABLE PEOPLE ON THE PLANET, UNCLE WILLIAM. MOST OF THEM MORONS, THE REST SCHIZOPHRENIC.
BUT ONLY ONE THAT IS BOTH AND AT THIS PARTY WITH THE PRESIDENT.
ARE YOU SURE, WILLIAM?
MARY-ANNE DOES NOT NEED YOUR HELP, MI.
snicker
SORRY.
PLEASE, THESE ARE FOR YOU. ANYTHING YOU NEED, JUST BUZZ AND ASK.
THEY ARE PAGERS. RAPHAEL'S RECEIVER SHOWS WHERE YOU ARE IN THE HOUSE.
SO YOU DO NOT HAVE TO WAIT. I WILL FIND YOU.
THANKS.
THANK YOU, MR. RAPHAEL.

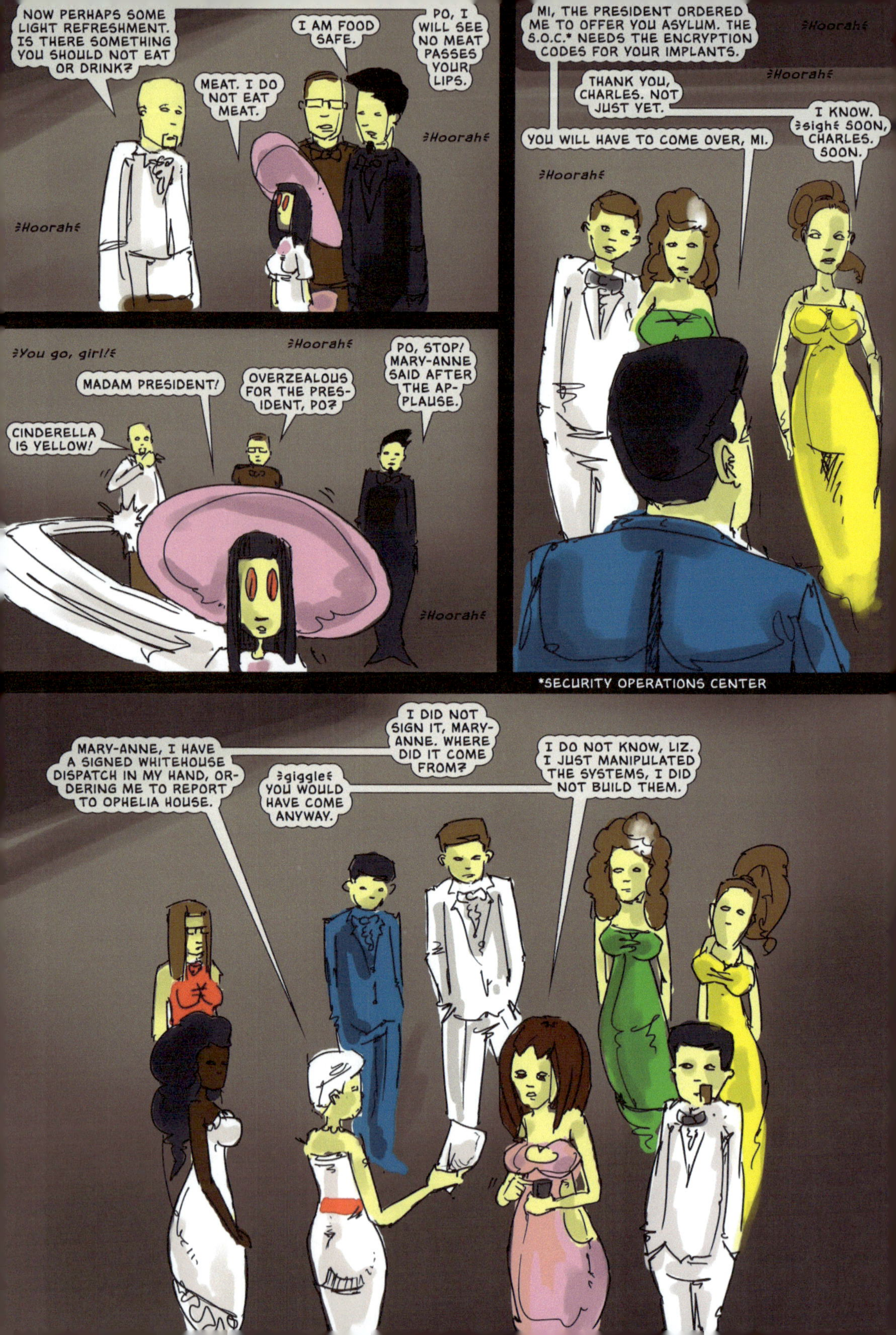
NOW PERHAPS SOME LIGHT REFRESHMENT. IS THERE SOMETHING YOU SHOULD NOT EAT OR DRINK?
I AM FOOD SAFE.
PO, I WILL SEE NO MEAT PASSES YOUR LIPS.
MEAT. I DO NOT EAT MEAT.
Hoorah
Hoorah
You go, girl!
Hoorah
MADAM PRESIDENT!
OVERZEALOUS FOR THE PRESIDENT, PO?
PO, STOP! MARY-ANNE SAID AFTER THE APPLAUSE.
CINDERELLA IS YELLOW!
Hoorah
MI, THE PRESIDENT ORDERED ME TO OFFER YOU ASYLUM. THE S.O.C.* NEEDS THE ENCRYPTION CODES FOR YOUR IMPLANTS.
Hoorah
Hoorah
THANK YOU, CHARLES. NOT JUST YET.
YOU WILL HAVE TO COME OVER, MI.
I KNOW. sigh SOON, CHARLES. SOON.
Hoorah
*SECURITY OPERATIONS CENTER
MARY-ANNE, I HAVE A SIGNED WHITEHOUSE DISPATCH IN MY HAND, ORDERING ME TO REPORT TO OPHELIA HOUSE.
I DID NOT SIGN IT, MARY-ANNE. WHERE DID IT COME FROM?
giggle YOU WOULD HAVE COME ANYWAY.
I DO NOT KNOW, LIZ. I JUST MANIPULATED THE SYSTEMS, I DID NOT BUILD THEM.

WOW! SHE IS BEAUTIFUL. I MEAN, WOW!
CHARLES.
I LEFT THEM ON THE TERRACE?
giggle THAT IS PO, CHARLES.
DO NOT WORRY, BARABARA. PO IS A FAN OF PAUL'S. giggle
MARY-ANNE!
LIZ, THROW YOUR SIGNED DISPATCH AWAY OR FRAME IT. YOU KNEW I WAS HANDLING OUR GUEST TRAVEL AR-RANGEMENTS.
IT IS MY JOB TO WORRY, MI. GAIL, WHICH ONE-OR IS IT BOTH OF THE PEOPLE WALKING WITH BREWSTER-IS NOT SAFE, AND WHY ARE THEY HERE?
WHAT DID YOU EXPECT, LIZ, AN INCIDENT?
WELL, I WAS A LITTLE CONCERNED.
WELL, YOU SHOULD NOT HAVE BEEN. BREWSTER, PHONE.
YES, MISS MARY-ANNE.

SO, PAUL FINGER PAINTED SHAPES LIKE THE ONES ON MARY-ANNE'S BRACELET AND SCROLL?
JUST ONE SHAPE ON THE BRACELET AND SCROLL. PAUL THOUGHT IT WAS HIS OWN ARBITRARY UNIQUE SHAPE. IT IS NOT.
MARY-ANNE'S BRACELET AND SCROLL? WHAT SHAPE?
TWO NEW PIECES IN MARY-ANNE'S ANCIENT ARTIFACTS OF SECRET CULTS COLLECTION. A SHAPE ON A BRACELET AND SCROLL, AND A SHAPE ON A WALL HANGING PAUL FINGER PAINTED ARE THE SAME SHAPE. PAUL BELIEVED HE CREATED THE SHAPE.
PLEASE EXCUSE ME, MADAM PRESIDENT. I WAS RUDE TO BE FORWARD. I AM SORRY.
THAT IS OKAY, PO. CALL ME LIZ.
I SEE MR. BREWSTER AND LADY ON TV TALK ABOUT YOU, MADAM PRESIDENT. LADY ON TV SAY, "YOU GO, GIRL".
WHAT IS HER OBSESSION WITH THE PAINTING?
PO SAYS SHE SEES MOVING IMAGES SHOWING WAYS FOR A MAN AND WOMAN TO TOUCH.
WE ARE ASSUMING PO SEES SOMETHING SEXUAL.
I WOULD SAY PORNOGRAPHIC FROM WHAT I HEARD MARY-ANNE EXPLAIN TO HER.
HMM, MENTALLY CHALLENGED AND POSSIBLY SEXUALLY PSYCHOTIC.
RELAX, WILLIAM. BARBARA WILL BE WITHIN FEET OF LIZ ALL NIGHT.
MARY-ANNE SAID SCHIZOPHRENIC. CHARLES, IS SHE SAFE TO BE NEAR LIZ?

NO ONE ELSE IS TO KNOW PO'S BACKGROUND. YOU MET AT THE GALLERY, SHE IS A FAN OF PAUL'S. I WILL BRIEF BARBARA. STATION MASTER, GET ME ANWAR ROLANDO.
NOBODY. LIZ NEEDS TIME OFF.
YES, SIR.
WHAT ABOUT LIZ?
THANKS, CHARLES.
LOVE YOU, CHARLES.
CHARLES? HMM.
YOU LIE, MR. BREWSTER?
ONLY TRUTH, MR. BREWSTER. EVERYTHING ELSE LIES.
WELL, LET US JUST SAY I DO NOT TELL ALL THE TRUTH, PO.
I COULD NOT HAVE SAID IT BETTER, PO.
HELLO PO, I AM CHARLES.
THANK YOU AND HELLO. I AM PLEASED TO MEET YOU, MR. CHARLES.
PO, DO YOU MIND IF I ASK YOU A FEW QUESTIONS?
EXCUSE ME, MR. LANGLEY, SIR. WHAT TYPE OF QUESTIONS?
PERSONAL QUESTIONS, PAUL. IS IT OKAY, PO?
OKAY, MR. CHARLES.

YOU CAN BE JUST PO. NO GRAND-MOTHER, PO.
NO GRAND-MOTHER, MR. ANDREW?
NO GRAND-MOTHER, PO. THINK ABOUT IT, PO.
OKAY, I THINK ABOUT IT, MR. ANDREW.
CHARLES IS IMPRESSIVE.
HE IS THE BEST SECURITY BUREAUCRAT IN THE WORLD.
I DID NOT KNOW BARBARA WAS ACTIVE.
JUST FOR OUR FAMILY. SHE--
OH, BARBARA, BY THE WAY, ZZ SENDS HER REGARDS.
ZZ? WHAT? WHY?
ZZ WISHES SHE HAD MADE THE CHOICE I MADE.
WHAT DO YOU MEAN, BARBARA?
ZZ, THE NANNY AND ENFORCER FOR A WEALTHY FAMILY. *chuckle* ZZ? NAH.
ANYTHING, WILIAM, RATHER THAN HAVING CHOSEN TO HAVE HER LIFE FILLED WITH DAYS OF BETRAYAL, WORK-RELATED SEX, AND DEATH. JUST A FEW OF THE RUNGS ON ZZ'S LADDER TO THE TOP.
ZZ IS WHAT I WOULD HAVE BECOME BUT FOR CHARLES. GET AWAY FROM HER--AWAY FROM THE E.A.I.C., MI.
BARBARA, YOU KNOW ZZ LIKE A BOOK. BUT IT IS NOT QUITE TIME FOR ME.
I KNOW CHARLES SPOKE TO YOU. IT HAS TO BE SOON, MI.

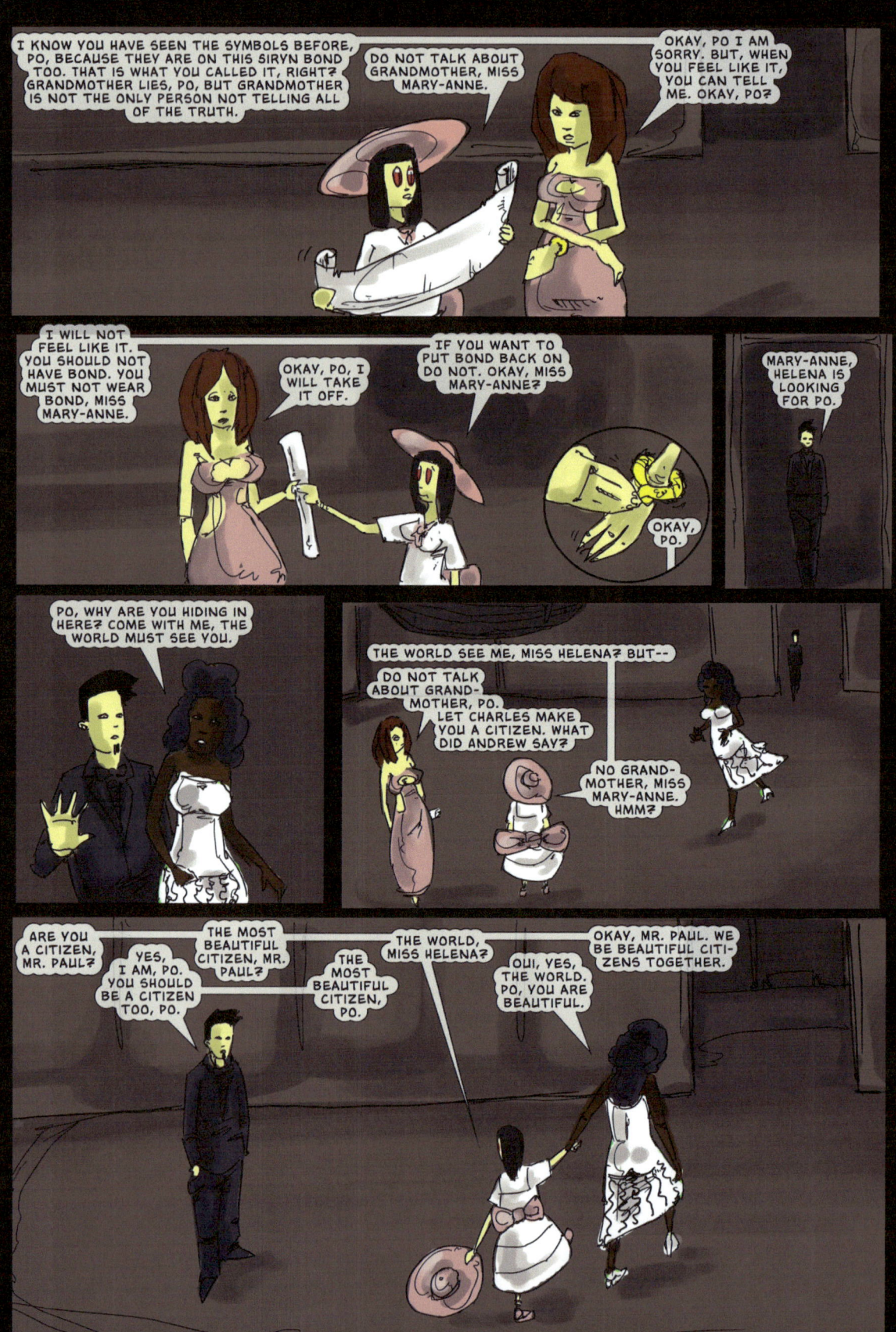

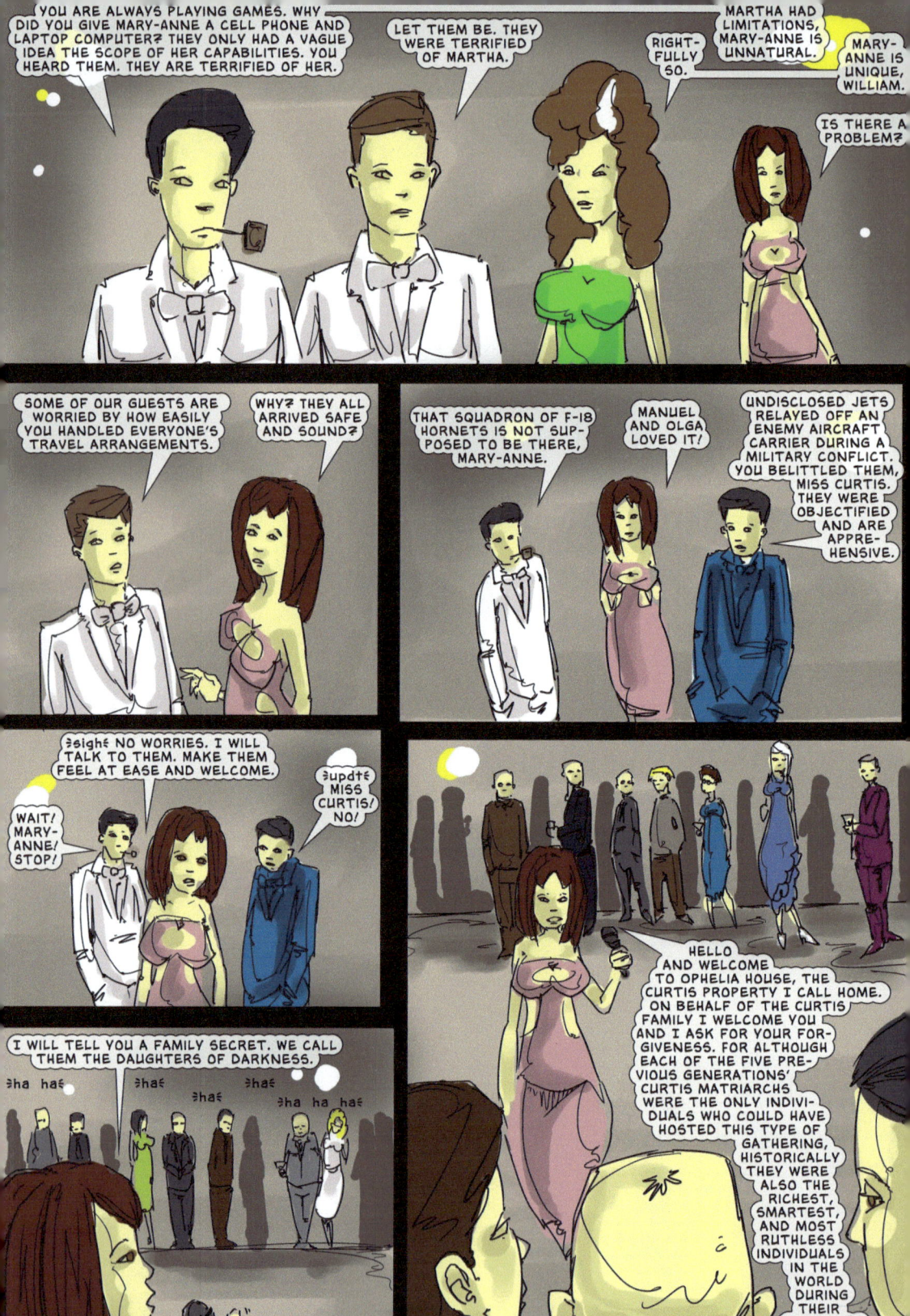

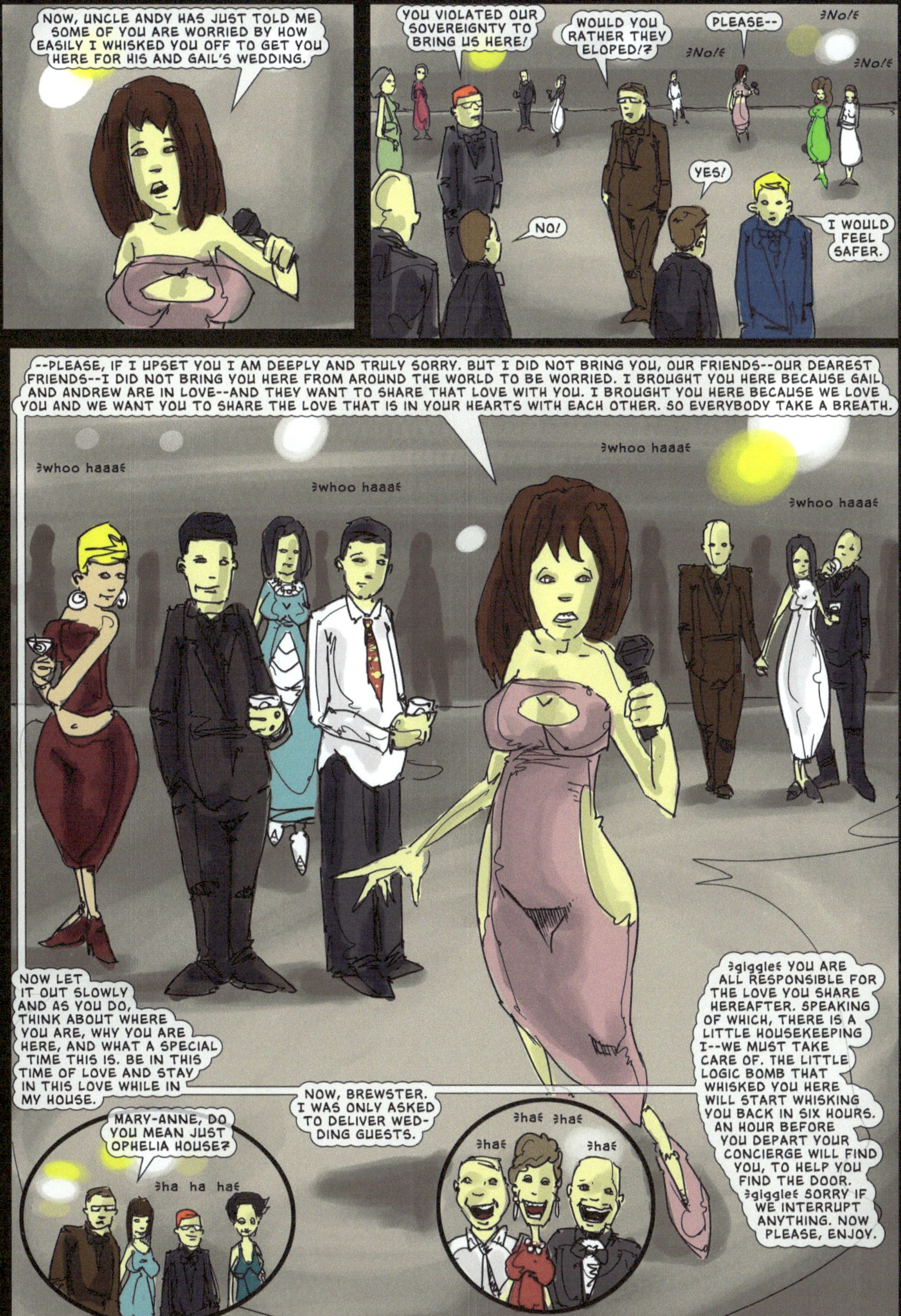

NOW, UNCLE ANDY HAS JUST TOLD ME SOME OF YOU ARE WORRIED BY HOW EASILY I WHISKED YOU OFF TO GET YOU HERE FOR HIS AND GAIL'S WEDDING.

YOU VIOLATED OUR SOVEREIGNTY TO BRING US HERE!

WOULD YOU RATHER THEY ELOPED!?

PLEASE--

ƎNo!Ɛ

ƎNo!Ɛ

ƎNo!Ɛ

NO!

YES!

I WOULD FEEL SAFER.

--PLEASE, IF I UPSET YOU I AM DEEPLY AND TRULY SORRY. BUT I DID NOT BRING YOU, OUR FRIENDS--OUR DEAREST FRIENDS--I DID NOT BRING YOU HERE FROM AROUND THE WORLD TO BE WORRIED. I BROUGHT YOU HERE BECAUSE GAIL AND ANDREW ARE IN LOVE--AND THEY WANT TO SHARE THAT LOVE WITH YOU. I BROUGHT YOU HERE BECAUSE WE LOVE YOU AND WE WANT YOU TO SHARE THE LOVE THAT IS IN YOUR HEARTS WITH EACH OTHER. SO EVERYBODY TAKE A BREATH.

Ǝwhoo haaaɛ

Ǝwhoo haaaɛ

Ǝwhoo haaaɛ

Ǝwhoo haaaɛ

NOW LET IT OUT SLOWLY AND AS YOU DO, THINK ABOUT WHERE YOU ARE, WHY YOU ARE HERE, AND WHAT A SPECIAL TIME THIS IS. BE IN THIS TIME OF LOVE AND STAY IN THIS LOVE WHILE IN MY HOUSE.

MARY-ANNE, DO YOU MEAN JUST OPHELIA HOUSE?

Ǝha ha haɛ

NOW, BREWSTER. I WAS ONLY ASKED TO DELIVER WEDDING GUESTS.

Ǝhaɛ Ǝhaɛ

Ǝhaɛ Ǝhaɛ

ƎgiggleƐ YOU ARE ALL RESPONSIBLE FOR THE LOVE YOU SHARE HEREAFTER. SPEAKING OF WHICH, THERE IS A LITTLE HOUSEKEEPING I--WE MUST TAKE CARE OF. THE LITTLE LOGIC BOMB THAT WHISKED YOU HERE WILL START WHISKING YOU BACK IN SIX HOURS. AN HOUR BEFORE YOU DEPART YOUR CONCIERGE WILL FIND YOU, TO HELP YOU FIND THE DOOR. ƎgiggleƐ SORRY IF WE INTERRUPT ANYTHING. NOW PLEASE, ENJOY.

PO LYN LEE
OPHELIA HOUSE
NEXT ISSUE

"SIRYN SISTERS"

IT IS A RITUAL DANCE FOR PO AND
MARY-ANNE. CEREMONIOUSLY GAIL PALMER
AND ANDREW CURTIS TAKE THEIR VOWS,
A BOND TO FOREVER RETURN. THE E.A.I.C.
BOARD WEIGHS ITS OPTIONS AND VOTES TO
TAKE HELENA'S BIRTHDAY GIFT THE DAY
AFTER. SOME BANDS DO NOT WANT TO PLAY
THE REFRAIN IN LADY LIBERTY'S SONG,
"THERE IS A PIECE OF CAKE FOR EVERYONE
AND A PIECE FOR THE WORLD."

CARLTON L. SAMPSON

POET, GRAPHIC NOVEL AUTHOR
CARLTON@POLYNLEE.COM
OTHER WORK AVAILABLE AT:
WWW.PHASCISTCLOWNS.COM


ANDREW L. WILLIS

AKA, THIOBIS THE ARTIST
FINE ART, SCULPTURE, ANIMATION,
MUSIC, AND AUTHOR.
ANDREW@POLYNLEE.COM
OTHER WORK AVAILABLE AT:
WWW.WAOOBAKEARTWORK.COM


COPY EDITORS TASHA, "THE MUSE," AND CAROL

OPHELIA HOUSE
BALLROOM

IT IS A RITUAL DANCE FOR PO AND MARY-ANNE. CEREMONIOUSLY GAIL
PALMER AND ANDREW CURTIS TAKE THEIR VOWS, A BOND TO FOREVER
RETURN. THE E.A.I.C. BOARD WEIGHS ITS OPTIONS AND VOTES TO TAKE
HELENA'S BIRTHDAY GIFT THE DAY AFTER. SOME BANDS DO NOT WANT TO
PLAY THE REFRAIN IN LADY LIBERTY'S SONG, "THERE IS A PIECE OF CAKE
FOR EVERYONE AND A PIECE FOR THE WORLD."

## NEXT ISSUE

# WWW.POLYNLEE.COM

www.ingramcontent.com/pod-product-compliance
Lightning Source LLC
Chambersburg PA
CBHW041538240626
47164CB00002B/48